RESPECT 4 ENDANGERED SPECIES

A collection of Short Stories

By Peggy Marceaux

ISBN: 978-1-956581-27-0

Erin Go Bragh Publishing
Canyon Lake, TX

Manufactured in the United States of America
Book Design by Kathleen's Graphics

Table of Contents

PEANUT BUTTER CUPS AND BABY WOOT'S

PEANUT BUTTER CUPS AND BABY WOOT'S

Table of Contents

PEANUT BUTTER CUPS AND BABY WOOT'S

Mr. and Mrs. Goldblum's were a fairly well-known, affluent family who lived in Dallas. They had a son, Levi, and a daughter, Ruth, both seven and three and a half respectively. Mr. Goldblum was an engineer, and Mrs. Goldblum a lawyer. Their son was a prodigy that they were very proud of; so proud that they bought him his own computer for the Montessori school he was attending, even a 3-D printer, in hopes that he would explore and create something they could be equally as proud of. To that end, they gave him *Carte Blanche* with the printer.

Levi had an insatiable appetite for gangster novels. He would read every description of every last item of clothing that they wore and every weapon that they wielded. His latest crime book was about Bonnie and Clyde.

"Hey, Ruth, why don't you play Bonnie Parker to my Clyde Barrow for Halloween?"

"Who ara day?" she asked.

"Oh, just some old timey gangsters," he answered her.

"Wha fo me?" asked baby Ruth.

"Baby Ruth's."

"Oh, I wov Baby Woots!" She exclaimed while clapping her tiny hands.

Then she said, "Otay, but I wan Baby Woots."

So, Levi worked out the logistics of creating Clyde's "whippet" – his shotgun, with the butt sawed off right after the handle, and printed it out on his 3-D printer. He was bummed it could only print a 12 gauge and not a 10 gauge, but, oh well, he had to settle. He bought himself a dark, three-piece, pinned-striped suit and fedora like Clyde wore; he bought Ruth an A-lined skirt with a loose top, a black beret and scarf, and a slip to wear scandalously on the outside of her clothing, just like Bonnie did. He bought her a cigar, just like Bonnie smoked, too.

"Dat's yucky," Ruth had said. So, he soaked that end in sugar water. He also bought lots of jellybeans to put in the bullet belt around Bonnie's waist. And, of course, they wore Bonnie and Clyde masks. When Halloween night came, they were off.

The first house they came to belonged to friends they'd visited at times. When they rang the doorbell, Mrs. Moron opened the door smiling, expecting to see normal trick or treaters. Instead, she encountered a miniature Bonnie and Clyde. She gasped.

Clyde had his "whippet" on her, handed her a money bag and said, "Put only your Reese's Peanut Butter Cups and Baby Ruth's in here, and nobody will get hurt. Otherwise, I'll fill you full of lead."

Only when she looked down and saw their tennis shoes and gauged their heights and approximate ages, could she see the little boy and the little girl in them.

Ruth pulled that nasty cigar out of her mouth and said, "Yeh, and wots of Baby Woots."

But, scared for her life with the way things had been going on in the news, and school shootings and all, she slammed the door on them. That called for Clyde to open fire on her door, peppering it with multi-colored jelly beans.

"Ah, I don wanna pay dis dame anymora," pouted Ruth. "I wan Baby Woots!"

Soo, the Morons pressed charges, the lawyer mom got them off, and Levi's dad took away the *Carte Blanche* for the printer; however, part of Levi's punishment was going back into the library and returning the book. He took advantage of that time to get another on the *Life and Times of Charles "Lucky" Luciano,* a Sicilian gangster boss from the thirties and early sixties. Levi also went by a convenience store on his way home to pick up two Baby Ruth's for his sister.

Reading at night after home-work, it took Levi only two nights to finish the book before he was ready to make "Lucky's" M1911 with his 3-D printer. It was a semi-automatic pistol that used .45 caliber bullets: in his case, at eight years old, he would be using jellybeans, of course. He was also ready to dress like "Lucky"; he took meticulous notes on what he wore from head to toe. The only thing he couldn't recreate was "Lucky's" physical appearance. It seems, once, when he was young, "Lucky" wasn't so lucky. He was trapped in a car where he was beaten, which caused permanent scars and a droopy eye. Levi couldn't even pretend he had a droopy eye.

That really bummed him because it was not like he didn't try.

Before long, Levi was wearing "Lucky's" black, felt fedora, his 3-piece suit made of very fine quality wool, though Levi couldn't have it tailored like "Lucky". He was wearing men's high-topped, dressed boots which looked like boats on him. He wore suspenders like "Lucky" did in his in his younger years, had a silk tie, and, like "Lucky," even sported a little pinky ring on his right hand. He was ready for his next adventure, whatever that might be. He talked to his sister about it, who wanted no part of it unless it would get her "Baby Woots."

He thought of robbing a bank, but it wasn't reasonable to assume they'd have candy.

"No. I'm sorry, Ruth, but I can't think who to hit up that would have candy."

"How 'bout dat cobeyunce stora you det dem fwom?"

His eyes lit up. "Oh, good idea!" *Now why didn't I think of that?* he wondered. "Let's do it before Mom gets home," he told her.

"Otay, wha I do?"

"Nothing much. Here, just hand them this money bag; I'll tell them what to put in it," Levi told her.

"Wha I need?"

"Nothing," he said.

They walked to the store where Levi waited until no one was in there, slipped a mask over his mouth and then entered, holding his pistol up at the employee. "This is a hold up. Just do what I ask you and nobody gets hurt." He waved to Ruth to give the man the bag, but she was at the shelf looking at all the different kinds of candy.

"Ruth! Give him the bag." Levi said.

"Wha bag?" She answered.

"The candy bag," he stated. "Pay attention."

She pouted and threw it to the employee.

"Fill the bag with all your Reese's Peanut Butter Cups and –"

"Baby Woots!" She hollered.

"—and Baby Ruth's," he said, "Or I'll fill you full of lead," he finished.

Once out of the store with the goods, Levi saw him reach for his phone, at which point he opened fire with his semiautomatic and raked the door and window with jellybeans. Levi had the employee ducking because he used only black jellybeans to more resemble real bullets. Nonetheless, they were jellybeans, so the store owner told their parents that all they wanted was monetary retribution. Still, Ruth had "Baby Woots" all over her hands. She was a happy little crook.

The Goldblum felt they needed to move because of Levi, so they changed their address to a nice area near Sea World in San Antonio.

Still, he had to be punished, so Levi was grounded, which meant he had to stay home, except he could return his book to the library, and could not use his printer for a month. He still went to school, of course, and, actually, at the library he returned Charles 'Lucky" Luciano in for Al Capone's story on the QT. He would be nine years old when he'd be making Capone's Colt .45 semiautomatic pistol and was ready to go on to something other than jellybeans.

He worked on what kind of bullets he could substitute for jellybeans, and came up with hard-shell, dark-chocolate-covered peanuts—or whatever kind of nut was the size of a .45 caliber bullet that wouldn't disintegrate as soon as it was struck by the pin. Levi was getting much more technical which didn't bode well for his obsession. He was trying to discuss the matter with Baby Ruth, who wouldn't be a baby for much longer

"Wha's a pin?" she asked.

"Well," Levi said, "the part that cocks the gun is called the hammer," and he showed her on "Lucky's" gun. "Then when you pull the trigger, the part that fires the jellybean out is called the pin. It slams into the back of the jellybean and makes it come out really fast."

"Oh," she said. "I don no wha utter tined o tandy yu tan use den."

Hmm, he thought. Ruth had always been his muse, so, now, it was back to the books, though the technical books would never discus candy. He would have to buy some different kinds of nuts and try them out in "Lucky's" gun, since it, too, was a .45. He would first have to make a silencer for the gun so he could practice shooting it out back, for he was sure his neighbors knew he was being punished. It would break the rules, but he was willing to do it to feed his obsession, which, by now, at nine years of age, going on ten, was in complete control of his life.

Again, he finished reading about Al Capone in two nights, being careful to hide the book under the bed at midnight each night. He took copious notes on clothing, head, foot wear and jewelry. He asked to have his hair cut like him, though he didn't say who the "him" was; his mother didn't like her little boy losing all his beautiful curls to look like a man in the 1930's. Since Capone was called Scarface, Levi cut his face in two places and came up with some plausible reason for his parents. He used Lucky's pinstriped woolen pants, but he needed a belt and a double-breasted suit jacket with wide lapels and a white hanker chief to go in the breast pocket. After arranging to buy an old timey chain and a clasp, he was ready to be "out of prison." His folks couldn't help but notice the huge "X" over the date on the monthly calendar.

"Okay," they said, "You're free, but no more making guns and accosting people with them!"

"Yes, Mom," he'd said, at which point he retired to his room to get to work on how to make Capone's Colt .45 semiautomatic.

As soon as he received his allowance, he was in the men's department store buying the remainder of the clothes he needed, like winged-tipped shoes and spats, but they had to order those since no one wore those anymore. He told them, "they are for a school play I'm in." They would be there by the end of the week, so, it was just a matter of getting the hard chocolate-covered almonds he'd decided on for bullets, and he'd be all set. Now what to hit up, and why? He thought and thought. No more candy to steal—*what else would be worth getting in trouble for?* the nine-year-old thought.

Then, it hit him: the carnival came to town where you can win teddy bears and candy just for hitting targets. He was so proud of himself he giggled and told Baby Ruth he was taking her somewhere special.

She giggled with excitement, too. By that time his shoes and spats were in.

"An Baby Woots?" she squeaked.

"We'll see," he had said.

When they had arrived, everyone laughed thinking he was a part of the show. Plus, it got him in free. In a way, he was, so he laughed too, thinking they'd change their tune soon enough. But, they didn't. In fact, they never did. When he made it to the shooting stand, they wanted him to use their rifles. Instead, he pulled out his Colt .45.

"Man," said the carnie, "you come fully decked out, don't you?"

"Yep," answered Levi.

The carnie spoke up again. "Well, what will you want if you hit any of the various targets?"

Though there were numerous stuffed animals any child would have loved, Baby Ruth jumped up and down demanding "Baby Woots! Baby Woots!"

"Aw, I'm sorry," said the carnie, "we don't have candy here." She pouted. "Don't you want this big, stuffed bear?"

She shook her head. "Onee Baby Woots." She crossed her arms, and big tears welled in her eyes.

Her brother said, "If I can hit all of your targets at the same time will you get some Baby Ruth's?"

"Sure, little man," said the carnie, "but I—"

That's all it took for Levi to open fire at the stand. He aimed with one hand and raked back the hammer with the other, making it sound more like continuous fire than a single pistol. When he finished, every last target lay flat, and even the carnie was chewing the chocolate-covered almonds that had ricocheted into his gaping mouth.

Levi and Baby Ruth left the carnival with lots of Baby Ruth's, which she was currently enjoying, and even a few Reese's Peanut Butter Cups thrown in for good measure, one of which Levi was peeling back for himself right then. They were already on their way home. The best part about it is they'd be home before Mom and Dad, so no more punishment; however, he needed to get to and from the library, too.

"Come on, Ruthie, walk a little faster," he urged.

"I gotsa little legs," she replied.

At the library he turned Al Capone in for Baby Face Nelson and John Dillinger. The cover of the

Nelson book said they were practically inseparable. He got home just before his mother pulled into the driveway, *thank goodness,* he thought.

"Did you both have a good day?" she asked them.

"Oh, yes Ma'am," Ruth stated with chocolate on her face.

Levi's face was flushed, but he said "Yes, Ma'am." too.

"Looks like Ruthie got back into her Baby Ruth stash," she observed.

"Uh, yeah," he remarked.

When Levi started to read that night, he noticed that all the gangsters wore about the same thing in the 1930's; he guessed it was the style of the times. They wore a finely, woven-3-piece, pin-striped, wool suit with wide lapels, and a fedora. Like his height of 5'5" Baby Face (Lester Gillis) had a short life. He "accidentally" shot a playmate in the jaw at 12, and stole a car at 13, which put him in the penal institution for 18 months. He met John Dillinger when he helped him break out of jail. Dillinger had somehow carved out a wooden gun that he stuck in the ribs of a jailer to make him cough up his gun. Though very young, Baby Face Nelson married and had two children before he was shot dead by the FBI at only 25. His wife, Helen accompanied him on most of his forays.

Nelson and Dillinger came up with fake names to visit a gunsmith in San Antonio named Hyman Saul Leh(b)man, who modified Colt .38's into super pistols for the Little Bohemia group and for "Machine Gun" Kelly. He didn't know he was working with gangsters, but he was. A super pistol was a pistol that could be made to be a machine (tommy) gun by just placing a 20-bullet clip in it, stabilizing the barrel by adding another handle in front, and having the shooter press the trigger and hold it down. It normally had only its six-shooter, revolving barrel, but Lehman changed all that. He was imprisoned for his part in the FBI murders that followed. Eliot Ness was in charge of the cases and helped\to bring the men down. He saw to it that, even though Lehman might be an innocent party in it, he was punished. The guns were getting more complicated for Levi to replicate, but it was a challenge he looked forward to.

It took Levi two weekends to make Nelson's .38 Super Colt automatic. He told his folks he was making a school project. Something about the flintlock pistol Davy Crocket used. He had to do it over and over again; it was always back to Lehman's diagrams. Finally, he had it, and he was super proud.

His folks celebrated his tenth birthday soon after that day. Ruthie was six now, so all her baby talk was gone, which made Levi sad, but she still did call baby Ruth's Baby Woots; he'd like to think just for him. He loved the .38 Super Colt automatic; its action was something he had never experienced. He couldn't wait to try it out on somebody. He'd have to change to a smaller "bullet" though—something like a chocolate covered peanut.

He met with Ruth on the evening before bed. "Hey, Ruth, do you want to go to the Sea World theme park with me?"

"Sure, but how?"

"It's not that far. I can ride my bike and you can sit behind me."

"Okay," grinned Ruth.

"We just need to do it tomorrow before Mom gets home." he said.

"And what about school?"

"I'll write us both notes," he finished.

"Cool," she said and hugged him. "Are we getting any Baby Ruth—I mean Woots?"

"Could be," and he smiled like he was holding a secret close to his chest.

The next morning, after his parents left for work, Levi and Ruth headed for Sea World, a miniature Baby Face and his sister pumping in on a bike.

Levi found his way to the concession stand and slipped off the bike, making sure to safely remove his sister before engaging the kick stand.

"My goodness," said the employee, "you re dressed for a show. Which is it?" she asked.

"The reenactment of gangster warfare," answered Levi.

"Where will that program be held? I haven't heard of it." the woman working the booth asked.

Oh, over by the knights in battle, he thought to say, but while it was so early, and few people were there yet, he thought it best to hold up now.

"This is a stick up. I need all your Reese's Cups and Baby Ruth's in this bag," and he threw her the bag.

The employee shied away with her hands up.

"Put your hands down. I don't want to draw any attention, that's why I haven't pulled my gun."

As soon as another worker asked if he could help, Levi asked for two sodas. He handed his sister the sodas, took the bank bag and thanked them kindly. In lieu of reimbursement, Levi took out Baby Face's .38 Super automatic and sprayed the concession stand with the Tommy machine gun's peanuts. Smashed chocolate peanuts covered everything.

Then, they jumped on the bike and pedaled out of there as fast as they could. They made it home before mom, thank goodness. Levi sat down and wrote them notes for school the next day right then, still, the concession hold up followed them home. Their parents were livid.

"Levi Goldblum, we can't believe you're still doing this!" said his dad. "You are grounded for the rest of the year!" He went into Levi's room, unplugged the 3-D printer and took it with him. He went into the garage and locked his bike with a big chain and a heavy padlock for which only he had the key.

His mom plopped a recipe book for Hershey's chocolate bars and Nestle recipe book for Nestle bars and said: "here now, read, and put your mind to making your candy in a legal way. If you keep going the way you are, pretty soon you'll be shooting real bullets, and we'll be visiting you in the penitentiary."

Then, they both left for work. Levi sat there for a minute. Ruth said, "Levi, I'll come help you get out of jail."

"Thanks, Ruthie."

Then Levi went into his parent's bedroom where he knew his dad kept his .38. revolver. He took 20 bullets for Baby Face's magazine that held twenty bullets and filled it up. He put on Baby Face's clothes and googled how to start a car without a key; his mom and dad had both their cars, but there were plenty in the driveways along his street. He went to a neighbor's and hot-wired the car. He drove it down to the first bank he could find and left the car running. Levi walked in, shot the security guard, gravely wounding him, and asked the teller for all the money in her drawer. He felt *exhilarated. So, this is how it feels*, he thought. He hustled back to the car and drove home. Levi took all the money and put it in an envelope marked "For Baby Woots" then stuffed it under Ruthie's mattress.

When his folks visited him in juvenile hall, they couldn't believe it. Where had they gone wrong? They couldn't look him in the eyes, but Ruthie could. Levi and Ruth smiled at one another. "Hi, lil sis;" he slipped her a Baby 'Woot,' "Hi, big bro," and she pushed him a Reese's Peanut Butter Cup.

LEROY DIMWIT THE NIT WIT

LEROY DIMWIT THE NIT WIT

LeRoy Dimwit woke 30 minutes earlier than he planned to be at Pap McElrath's Ranch, because he had to put the ball of his truck under the hitch coupler. He always had a dickens of a time doing that. He'd back his truck up too far to the left, or too far to the right. He always knew when he was right on it because he would feel the hitch bang into the tailgate. Then he'd have to go out and look how much he could back up or go forward. That was an experience, in itself; he'd move it back too far or get another bang. Needless to say, his old '55 Chevy took quite a beating.

He finally pulled onto Highway 90A in Belmont, going east toward Gonzales; he wanted to be at the ranch in thirty minutes, or so, waiting for his tractor. Travis had borrowed it to mow Pap McElrarh's Ranch while there was no dew on the ground. With every little brake or lurch, his trailer lagged or hit his truck, which happened a lot since his truck was a standard. LeRoy Dimwit didn't understand the workings of a hitch well enough to realize that the size of the ball on his truck was too small for the coupler.

Finally there, LeRoy parked his truck and trailer on the left side of the road. There was maybe five yards of grass before the fence began; it was a beautiful piece of property with well-manicured, rolling hills. LeRoy lay his head back, and, before long, he was asleep. He had no idea he'd be before a judge later that day.

"Yer honor, Sir, ah c'n splain," he said, to the judge of Guadalupe County. "Ye see ah wuz parked by de side of Highway 90A, 'tween Belmont and Gonzales, waitin' fer Travis ta finish mowin' dis here ranch wit ma tractor 'fore it gots too hot. It had been dryer dan a witch's tits fer months, so we knowed it'd be dry 'nough ta mow at dat time. Anyway, ah gots dere 'bout five tirty, and, ah don't knowed, ah tink de drone a de tractor put me ta sleep. Den sum kind a gruntin' noise woke me up. Ah oped ma eyes and, on de left, ah seed dis here buck and doe gittin' it on. Dat's when ah seed dis utter buck haulin' ass right cross de street, comin' at me. Ah start ta tink, hell, he's gonna hit me. An, ah'll be damned ifn he didn't! Ah don't tink he e'en seed ma truck. He had his nose full of doe twat. He jumped up, an' ah tink he caught hisself in my aerial somehow, an', it flipped him. He put two tine holes in ma hood! Here ah am wid 3 deer bunched up on me. So what am ah s'pose ta do ta warn people 'bout dat? Ah'm gonna ta flash ma lights right? Well, dats sactly what. ah done. 'Fore ah knowed it dis here cop, ah mean officer, is wantin' ta write me a ticket fer warnin' people 'bout his speed trap. Hell, ah ain't e'en knowed he had no speed trap. How was ah s'ppose ta knowed dat? He come in ta set it up after me. Den ta make matters e'en worse, de car comin' at me slams on her brakes, which makes de truck b'hind her slam inta her, and den a sports car b'hind him slam inta him. Now, it seems, de speed car's man is lookin' fer somebody ta sue."

"And what about your trailer having no lights, Mr. Dimwit?" The judge asked him.

"Oh dat. Yessir, ah gots trailer lights. Ah jest haven't put dem on yet."

"If they're not on, you don't have them, Mr. Dimwit. I suggest you put them on before you use that trailer again."

"Oh, yessir, ah will."

"Now, what about that Winchester 30-30 you had laying by your side, Mr. Dimwit? You aiming to get yourself a buck from the road?"

"Oh no. Sir, ah c'n splain dat, ta. Ye see, we gots wild hogs eatin' us out a home and house out here. Ah figured ifn one crossed de road, ah could take it out fer all a us."

"You can't shoot from the road, Mr. Dimwit," the judge told him.

"Not e'en a wild hog?"

"Not even a squirrel," the judge concluded.

Dimwit looked at the judge with wide eyes, like it was the first time he ever heard of such nonsense. The country boy in him told him he'd have to see about that.

"Ifn ah shot a squirrel with a 30-30 there'd be nothin' left a 'em," and he chuckled.

The judge just stared at him. "You have a license to hunt, Mr. Dimwit?" The judge further inquired.

"No Sir. ah'm not huntin' so what ah needs a license fer? Ah was only talkin' 'bout wild hogs. Ye don't needs no license fer dem."

Dimwit thought of his buddies Shuggy and the Robinson boys, and how they hunted deer and what not from the "county lease" in Leesville. How he was glad he didn't have his spotlights in his truck; about that deer he hit in the head with his truck in the middle of the night; and how he took it to Billie Gus' to string it up; and how Billie Gus taught him to cut around the legs of the deer, tie the hide to the ball of his truck, and pull it all off with the truck. Sure made matters simpler. That was the country way. *He probably wuld have gots a ticket fer all a it 'cept the hide part. But it wuz his way, and he wudnt't gonna change dat,* he thought.

The bang of the gavel brought him out of of his reverie. "That'll be $250. Next case."

"$250? Whar am ah gonna git dat?" He asked.

"Next case!" the judge said, emphatically.

LeRoy left the courthouse feeling pretty dejected. Where in the world was he going to come up with that kind of money? He talked to his hunting friends, the Robinson brothers, the next time he met them on the "county lease", which was really County Rd. 121.

"Whar wuld ye guys git $250?" he asked. "Ya knowed ah ain't made outta money."

It didn't take Shuggy long to come up with the idea that Dimwit needed to get him an albino deer. "We have a few out here in these woods. I've seen 'em at times, jest never could get a good bead on one. Their hides go for at least that amount of money."

There was hope for Dimwit yet. So, he and the Robinson boys took their spotlights and went looking for one that night. They saw some regular white-tail in their spot lights for most of their hunt. Then, right near the end of the brush, Dimwit saw what looked to be a white deer's shoulder and body. He never saw its eyes. Hell, he didn't care if it was a doe or a buck; so he took aim and shot. There was the biggest, most agonizing noise that followed:

"OOUUUCCCHH!!!" The officer stood up and grabbed hold of his rear.

Dimwit froze. All the boys froze. Then the Robinson boys noticed a deputy sheriff's car parked across from them. They hadn't noticed it before because they were concentrating on the brush on the left side of the road. They jumped in their truck and sped off, leaving Dimwit there to face the consequences.

Dimwit had this strong desire to run, too, but his feet wouldn't budge. They were frozen in place. When the officer saw him, he told him to, "Please call for an ambulance."

"Ah don't have no phone, sir."

"Then use —ooohhh—my radio in the car. Please hurry!"

"Ah don't knowed how ta." Dimwit said, feeling helpless.

"Just pick up the receiver on the hook and say 911. Hurry!" the officer said, obviously in pain.

Dimwit called for an ambulance, remained there for the sheriff to be taken away, and then walked to Billie Gus' to get his truck and drive back to Belmont. Instead of taking care of his $250 debt, he knew he would only be adding more to it.

"So," said the judge, "what brings you back in here, uh--" and he looked at the ticket for a name, "is it Dimwit?"

Dimwit lowered his head. "Yessir," he said.

"And, can you explain this one as readily as you could your last one?"

"Yes, Sir, ah c'n splain, Ah was tryin' ta kill a albino deer ta pay ma det ta de courthouse," said Dimwit.

"In the middle of the night? With a spotlight? Well, that's no explanation at all. What you did was spotlight from the road, and on top of that, you shot an officer." The judge banged his gavel down. "That'll be $3500 and 6 months in jail; 3 for the delinquent fines and 3 for shooting the officer."

Whar ah'm gonna git dat kind a cash? Well, meybe ah can hit up de bank one tam and den ne'er do it agin, he thought.

So after serving his six months, he cased out the banks around and decided he wanted to rob a small bank, like Nixon's.

"Hey, Shuggy, did ah heared ya say ya bot a AK-47 not long ago? What fer?" he asked.'

"Oh, you know—to fool around with—shoot at beer cans and the like." Shuggy answered.

"Mind ifn ah borrow it fer a day? Ah'd like ta do de same."

"Alright, but it's got a hair trigger and lots of fire power, so be careful with it." Shuggy added. "It uses a .308 bullet, but I'll give you a loaded clip cuz we left you stranded with that sheriff." Shuggy told him.

That was the first time Shuggy referred to the incident with the sheriff, and he appreciated him suggesting they may have been at fault for any of that.

So, Dimwit got the gun and checked out where the bank was, but didn't dare go inside. He didn't ask what a hair trigger meant or lots of fire power. He didn't understand why they had to put a clip in the gun and what all those bullets Shuggy put in there were about. He just wanted to scare the clerk into giving him some money. He bought a mask that pulled down over his whole face with peep holes for his eyes. He thought, *Dis shuld do*, got his AK-47 and drove down to the bank. He put his mask on, opened his squeaky door and got out of his truck with the gun, then slammed the door. His peep holes turned and he had to turn them back. He entered the bank and realized it had a security officer. He hadn't counted on that. When the officer pulled a gun on him, Dimwit got rattled. His peep holes turned again, and his nervousness caused his finger to touch the rigger, Ak-47 bullets shot everywhere, mostly in the ceiling, scaring Dimwit half to death. The gun raced through the clip until it was empty—patrons and employees hit the floor and hid behind counters. The officer collared him, and the gun, and hauled them both to jail. In his mind, Dimwit kept seeing his debt soar, and Shuggy mad at him for getting him in trouble with the law. He was hauled before the judge, yet again.

"Mr. Dimwit, this time you are using an assault rifle. Have you anything to say about *that?*" The Judge was miffed.

"Yes, Sir. Wuz a assault rifle?"

"Oh, come now, Mr. Dimwit you can't tell me you don't know what an assault rifle is," he said staring him down.

"Ah dunno, Sir." Dimwit answered.

"Well, you need to google it before you use another one," the judge told him.

"Wuz 'google' mean?" The judge rolled his eyes.

"That'll be six months in jail again. $3500. Next case," he said, and hammered his gavel down.

Dimwit gulped. While he was serving his time, he got the answers he needed. Still, there was this thing called "debt" hanging over his head. Where would he come up with the money to pay the $7250, he now owed the courts. He decided he would hit up a gun store in Nixon. He had a window cutter that would do the trick. It would get him in the store through the front glass door, and then he could pick out the gun he wanted and get the ammo, too. All he had to do was be cool, not attract attention, and be quick. He entered the store during normal hours to look around and told the proprietor he was just there to check out his pistols. Things looked in order. *It would be a piece of cake,* he thought.

So, one night, pretty soon after his jail time, Dimwit quietly pulled into the gun store parking lot. He didn't even shut his door so as not to attract attention. He took his glass cutter and cut enough of a size of glass for him to fit through, then entered the store. He searched for an AK-47 hanging on the wall, because that's what he had some experience with. Then, he got a box of .308 caliber ammo and a clip. With these in hand, he made his way out of the store and back to his truck. When he slammed the door to the truck someone saw him and called the law. The sheriff beat him home and arrested him for one count of breaking and entering and another count of robbery. Now he was ready to hit another bank.

When he appeared before the judge this time, the judge was fed up with him.

"Dimwit", he said. "Why can't you stay out of trouble?"

"Sir, ah c'n splain, ah owe de court so much money ah'm ahways lookin' fer ways ta pay it back." Dimwit looked so sincere and pathetic standing there that even the judge felt sorry for him.

"Let's see if we can get you on our road crew until you've paid the money back. For breaking and entering and robbery that would be a fine of $3000." The judge said and banged his gavel. "Next case."

Dimwit's mouth dropped open. *Ah'll be workin' de roads fer de rest a ma life*, he thought.

On the first day, the road crew gave him a yellow hard hat and a green vest. His job that day was to mix the tar and gravel they gave him that would be used to fill potholes. They gave him a bucket full of gravel and a bucket of tar. You'd think it couldn't be that difficult, but Dimwit got more tar on himself than he did in the bucket of gravel. He also had a hard time mixing it. The paddle they'd given him made it hard to stir. So, he had lumps of gravel mixed with tar and gravel without tar. When they were ready to pour it into the pothole, it was a mess. He had to rake the loose gravel out and try again. It was never better. So, they looked for another job for him.

They came up with him being the flag man; standing there holding a sign for traffic to proceed slowly or stop. What could be hard about that? But it was disastrous. Once, he told the traffic to go before the pilot car had come through with the oncoming traffic. Naturally, that was a near head-on collision with the pilot car and could have been a catastrophic collision with the oncoming traffic. They had to move Dimwit again, but, where to? They didn't dare let him run any of the machinery. They decided to give him a rake and let him smooth out the gravel they put in the potholes. That was harmless. But at $18 an hour, they needed to make him more useful.

They put him on drainage problems, and major sinkholes, but he fell into them. So, they tried putting him in charge of taking care of manholes; but he fell into them, too, and they had to get him out of the sewers too often, so, they assigned him to putting down and picking up orange cones and barrels. He got hit by a car doing that, which amounted to a brief hospital stay. They didn't dare put him on bridges, so he was relegated to picking up carcasses hit by cars in the middle of the night.

Phew, he thought. *Ah ain't gonna do dis no mo.*

The next day, Dimwit didn't show up for work. He was considered a fugitive from the law. He owed a bunch of money and gave up on his court-appointed job to get that cash. Now he'd have to go back to his old ways and steal it.

Dimwit decided he'd have to hit up a bigger bank because they would have more money. So, he checked out Wells Fargo in Seguin. But, he wasn't sure when their coach was coming in. He couldn't very well go in and ask them; that would be a dead giveaway. He always saw on *Gunsmoke* and the like that that's when their biggest stash of cash would come in. He thought it best that he hit it up first, before it made its way to the bank; that would take care of the security guard. But, as long as he waited, day after day, it never arrived. *Maybe it cames at night,* he thought. Finally, the time came when he had to go ahead without the wagon. He had his AK-47 and this ridiculous clip filled with ammo; he had his masked pulled down over his face with the peep holes where his eyes could see; he had practiced with the gun so it wouldn't spook him, and he entered the bank looking for the security guard. He saw one before he entered and disarmed him. He told the teller and everyone else he wasn't there to hurt them, but that he just needed money. He got his money and left the bank. *Finally, he could pay off his court costs,* he thought, as he got in his '55 Chevy, he slammed the door shut and chugged his way back home to Belmont; the security guard watching him until he was out of sight.

"Mr. Dimwit, you are becoming, a nuisance. I thought I left you on the road crew," the judge scowled at him.

"Yes, Sir, ah can splain dat."

"Well, you'd better do a damn good job," said the judge.

"Yes, Sir. Well everthan dey gives me ta do wuz a disasser. De las ting was pickin up ole road kill. It stunks bad, Sir."

"Well, Dimwit, what do you expect? Prim roses? It's a labor man's job," the judge defined.

"Yes, Sir."

"I can't think how else to help you out with these court costs. You need to keep your nose clean and get on our monthly plan. That's the best I can do for you." The judge banged his gavel and said, "$4,000 fine. Next case"

Dimwit was crushed. *More debt,* he thought. Dimwit didn't understand what his nose had to do with any of this, but he made sure he blew it clean every day. He didn't trust the government enough to get on their monthly plan, so that was out of the question. He failed at robbery for little things he didn't think about, so he needed to think of everything before he tried next time. He thought the security guard had seen him watching for the Wells Fargo coach, and that's how he was found out. He needed to hit up a place without a coach.

Dimwit found this bank called Pioneer Bank in San Marcos. It was a long way from Belmont, but he thought his old '55 Chevy would make it just fine. He liked the name of the bank, and from what he learned of it, there was no coach involved. Just these things called Zelle, ATM and apps that he never heard of, and he didn't have to know about. All he wanted was cash anyway. So, he made sure he had cased it and knew he couldn't get in any anymore trouble if he robbed it. He picked a day to go, got his gun, ammo and mask ready and headed north. When he arrived, he chugged his way into the bank parking lot and approached the entrance, first to disarm the security guard and then to go up to the teller. He told the employees and patrons what he told the ones at Wells Fargo, then he got his cash and was outta there. He jumped into his Chevy truck and chugged back to Belmont. He started to count out what he owed the court when there was a loud bang on the door. To his amazement he heard them identify themselves as "police."

Dimwit hid the money, the gun and then opened his door. Two policemen had pistols drawn and were aiming them at him. "LeRoy Dimwit?" They asked."

"Yes, Sirs," Dimwit said, with his hands up.

"Someone reported your '55 Chevy leaving the Pioneer Bank after a hold up. The suspicion falls on you. Now we need all that money back." Dimwit reluctantly gave it back to them, was then handcuffed and put into their squad car. This was the first time he felt like a criminal.

Ma truck, Andrew thought. *Dat's wuz been givn' me away.*

"Dimwit," the judge said. "I'm sick of seeing your face. Next time I do, I'm throwing you in the pen for a long time." he said and slammed his gavel down. "$5,000 fine. Next case"

When Dimwit left, he felt utterly dejected. There was no way he could get all that money back without stealing it, and it seems like everything he did got him found out. The pen might be the best thing after all, but he just had to try one more time since, he now knew what all told the law it was him doing the stealing. He chose JPMorgan since he knew it was a big bank with lots of money. He loaded his clip, picked up his AK-47 and mask with the peep holes and drove to the bank in San Marcos. He parked his truck in the *back* of the bank instead of the front parking lot. He put his mask on and pulled the peep holes over his eyes. As he entered the bank, he didn't see a security guard, then, one stepped out around the counter with another assault rifle. That scared Dimwit nearly to death. He whirled and ran out of the bank, around to the back of it and jumped into his truck. He turned the key and got a weird noise he only gets when the battery is dead. He couldn't believe it. *Not now,* he thought.

"No, Sir, ah cain't splain dis one," he told the judge, his head down.

"That'll be two years in the penitentiary," the judge said, and slammed his gavel down. "Next case."

And just like that, Dimwit's life changed forever.

Dimwit was assigned to the Kyle Correctional Center to serve out his sentence. About six months into it, he came down with a bad case of COVID and was released to finish out his sentence in his home through the Compassionate Act and the Executive Clemency Act. It took Dimwit a long time to get over COVID, but he was glad to be able to do it at home. His friends had to help feed him and get his medicine, though, and he had very few friends left. At least he wouldn't have to pay all that money to the court now, so that was off of his shoulders. Finally, he could begin to live his life all over again.

The first thing Dimwit did was answer an ad in the Belmont Gazette about someone wanting to buy an AK-47. He sold it, along with its clip and the bullets. It wasn't long before he was facing that same judge again. It seems the buyer had a rap sheet an arm's length long.

"Yes, Sir, ah can splain:" Dimwit told him. "Ah wuz jest tryin' ta sell a gun, and a fellar wuz wantin' ta buy it. How am ah s'ppose ta knowed he wuz a crimnal?"

"Well, Dimwit, I suggest you do a background check on who you are selling to next time," the judge said. Banged his gavel, "$500 fine. Next case," he said.

Dimwit saw his life flash before his eyes again. *Dis cain't be happnin' agin*, he thought. He saw red.

Dimwit went home and took out his .30 -.30. He loaded it and walked directly to his truck. He pulled the squeaky door open, got inside and slammed it shut. He drove to the courthouse and entered. His gun sounded through the metal detector, but Dimwit pointed the gun at everyone who tried to grab him. He walked into the courtroom, put a bead on the judge who said, "What is the meaning of this?" and fired off two rounds before anyone could stop him. The judge was killed instantly.

Dimwit tried to fight off the security guards that tried to stop him, but eventually had to let them take him and his rifle. Still, it felt good to be rid of that man and his control over his life. He'd rather go to prison than hear another word come out of his mouth. And, prison is definitely where he was heading. Only, instead of sending him back to Kyle, they sent him to ADX Florence in Colorado, where they sent prisoners most capable of violence against other inmates or the staff. Dimwit hardly thought that was fair, but he had no choice in the matter. Still, he thought he could try to get out anyway. There was only a total of 341 inmates; surely, they had suggestions for him to try.

While there, he tried the John Dillinger trick of carving a bar of soap into a gun. He couldn't quite get the hang of it since he couldn't get hold of a knife. He was told to take a kitchen butter knife and stick it up his sleeve, but when he did that, it fell out going back to his cell. Dimwit just couldn't get the nit wit out of his way.

So, he was placed in isolation: three months in total darkness. Later, when he was let out, he couldn't stop squinting, his eyes were so sensitive to the light. It was the worst thing that had ever happened to him, but he came out just in time for his first conjugal visit. Since he had no wife or girlfriend, the warden hired him a girl. He was given a pill for her, a rubber for himself, shut up in a private room and told to "enjoy.

"Hey, Dimwit, how'd it go?"

Dimwit said, "Not ta good. De pill falls out and the rubber tores. Beside, dat, ah culdn't git it up"

The jailer laughed. "Oh, you dim wit, she's supposed to take the pill by mouth."

"Oh," Dimwit said.

"Well, you have three weeks to practice getting it up. She visits again then," his jailer said. He cracked up laughing, locked him back up and passed him his food.

Betty Sue had asked LeRoy if there was anything he wanted her to bring him, and he said, "Yeh, a bar of soap dat looks like a gun. "

She asked, "Ivory, Dove, Dial,--?"

"Don' cared how it gud it smells. Jest one dat looks like a gun," he said.

She told him she could bring it next time in her under wear. The night, when the next time came, he had her take the pill by mouth and managed to put on the condom without tearing it. He also managed to "get it up." He later told his jailer that was the best five minutes of his life. The jailer just shook his head pitifully at LeRoy. "She took the pill by mouth before or after you screwed her?" asked.

"'Fore." Dimwit proudly proclaimed. The jailer laughed. "Well, I guess Betty Sue is a dim wit, too, because it's a morning after pill," and he kept laughing.

Dimwit was madder than a wet hen whose chick was in the mouth of a coyote.

"Ye ain't ne'er told me dat!" Dimwit shot back.

"Oh, wait til the boys hear this one," the jailer walked away laughing.

Later that night, Dimwi stuck the soap gun in his jailers back. "Gi'e me yer gun," Andrew told him.

The jailer had no choice but to disarm himself. When Dimwit slipped down the stairs to go outside, his jailer radioed to the rest of the staff, and the riflemen in the tower what had happened. But he told them, "It's just Dimwit. He'll hang himself somehow, so don't shoot."

Sure enough, when the warden unlocked the door for Dimwit to go outside, he started climbing the fence. The warden and most of the jailers followed him out. When he got stuck on the barbed wire he had to get over before he came to the razor wire to get out of there, they all cracked up laughing at him. The tower had the spotlight on him, watching what would happen next. Well, as his jailer foresaw, Dimwit got hung up on the barb wire and couldn't go any farther. After laughing for what seemed like forever, the men in the tower came down and forced him to give up his weapon before they'd take him down. It was just another nit wit moment.

The warden told him the staff all feel that prison is "Dimwit proof, and that he needs to stop trying to escape. Besides he only has three more weeks of his prison sentence to serve before he can get out."

Dimwit looked up at him, surprised. "Tree mo weeks. Dat's all?"

"That's all," the warden stated.

Dimwit sat back on the bed of his jail cell and couldn't believe he had miscounted so badly. It never occurred to him that the warden and his staff wanted him out of their hair.

"Only tree mo weeks, and ah'm a free man. Wow." He lay back on the bed with his hands behind his head and plotted out what he would do when he got out.

On the day he was released, Dimwit went home, got his old truck and drove it down to a gun show. He bought an AK-47, ammo and clips with a false ID. He got back into his truck and chugged all the way to the Colorado penitentiary. LeRoy hid his gun and told the security guard at the entrance he was coming in to visit his friend, Virgil, in block 8, cell 24. Once in, he got out of his truck and put the extra clips in his pocket. He began to open fire, first on the tower, then on the staff as they ran out to see what was going on, and how they could help. Once they were all dead, he went in and freed all the prisoners.

Later, in San Quintin, when he was asked why he did it, he told them, "Cuz dey always laffed at me and took me fer a nit wit. Ah'm a country boy. Dere ain't nuttin' wrong wit dat. De law ain't ne'er been a friend to me, or tried ta protect me, and **dat's** what's wrong. Not wit **me.** 'Sides, ah kinda like shootin' dat AK-47."

Peggy Marceaux

Buzz of Malta Meets Mrs. Peregrine of Gozo

This short story of Buzz and Mrs. Peregrine came from a prompt on the Maltese Falcon.

Buzz of Malta Meets Mrs. Peregrine of Gozo

Chirp, chirp, screech. Stoop. A Maltese falcon could descend upon a whole bird and engulf it in one collision. The fastest animal on earth, it could stoop at 200 or more mph. It didn't need a language; all it needed was a target, some height to get started, and its speed.

People, on the other hand, needed a language. The Maltese language was spoken in Sicily by indigenous people who were divided into Greek-rite Christians and Muslims. Their vocabulary has accrued massive amounts from Sicilian and Italian, into a Maltese that is the multi-cultural conglomeration of Sicilian, Arabic, Latin and Semitic languages. Before its independence in 1964, its women wore the ghonnella, a traditional dress of Maltese modesty that gradually disappeared in the 1960s. Now, they have a little more freedom with dress and speak Maltese, a language descended from Siculo-Arabic, an extinct dialect of that language. Arabic was spoken to a lesser degree than English and French. Since then, Maltese, or Malti, has become its national language.

When it came to women, Malta fell woefully short, both socially and politically. Socially, the Catholic Church was of the mind, that, if they kept them under their thumb (and their husbands'), they could keep them uneducated and use them as baby machines, for, the more parishioners the better. Politically, it was only after Archbishop Conzi left office in 1975, that women would have a chance getting into Parliament. At that, only three ran: Agatha Barbara, Evelyn Bonaci and Anne Ferrante. Agatha Barbara would become President of Malta in 1982. When universal suffrage came to Malta in 1947, the country could produce only two women. Even New Zealand had every adult female of every ethnicity voting in 1893. When women are stymied, whether by race or religion, it takes them a long time to catch up.

Malta the archipelago, itself, sits between Sicily and North Africa. Its other two islands are Gozo, the home of Mrs. Peregrine the falcon, and Camino, housing several fortresses, megalithic temples and historic sites. With a half a million people making up all of Malta, it is the tenth smallest nation, but it provided strategic naval help to the Allied Forces during WW II. It has been ruled by Greeks, Phoenicians, Aghlabids, Arabs, Muslims, Romans, Moors, the Knights of Saint John, the French and the British, just to name a few, but, it is known for much more than a diversity of courageous people; its falcons have also been a "flying force:" on the archipelago.

Since their near extinction, of the 3,000 peregrine falcons, 2,000 came back to live on Gozo Island in the Ggantija, a megalithic temple on the archipelago. They were under the leadership of Mrs. Peregrine, a magical bird who could turn herself into a beautiful woman at will, which she used for her primary focus during WW II: to win the war for the city-state of Malta. Gozo had the island of Camino between it and the largest island of Malta. Comino had only three people living there permanently, so the falcons had free reigns in the air. Comino was crowded with tourists for the spring and summer months. They came to see the Blue Lagoon, but that only put traffic on the sea. There was also a walled off battery built by the Knights of St. John around 1715 for tourists to peruse, but walking on Comino was long and hot, so not many tourists would not choose that over the coolness of snorkeling or scuba diving.

As well, since falcons mated for life, and the male was only one-third the size of the female, her mate could hardly exert any force over Mrs. Peregrine, leaving her to seduce anyone she so chose, even if it was Rommel and Mussolini. They were, after all, merely men, and men loved to wage war. At the moment they were destroying her beautiful home. She used her magic to coerce them into compromising positions. In actuality, she was more attracted to Buzz than to her own mate, so, she left everything else to him

Buzz was a peregrine falcon who had flown through the gauntlet of the British/Maltese firing at the Axis German Luftwaffe and the Italian Regia Aeronautica (Air Force) when he was young. He lost a few tail feathers and one wing was shorter than the other; aside from that, and losing his left eye, he was in good shape. The Maltese won the prestigious King George Cross for their heroic struggles and repeated attacks during WW II. Buzz felt as though he earned that Cross, as well. From 1940-1943, Fascist Italian Dictator Benito Mussolini and German Commander Erwin Rommel tried to siege Malta because of its close proximity to their supplies in Africa. Buzz tried to get a bead on both men and squirt a shot of excrement in both of their faces. "Bull's Eye!" he shouted twice. "*Shite!*" Rommel exclaimed. "*Merda!*" yelled Mussolini angrily. He enjoyed that as much as he did squirting the new Archbishop of Malta, Mikiel Conzi in 1944. "Bull's eye, again," he said. "*Cacas!*" proclaimed the Archbishop, horrified. *One eye hasn't disabled me at all,"* he thought arrogantly.

Buzz gathered his cast of raptors at the Ghar Dalam to stoop some altar boys and the Archbishop during one Ash Wednesday. He let them bring their mates along because they only gathered at mating season. Otherwise, they were solitary birds. It was rather unsetting talking to falcons who were so distracted, but it was the nature of the birds. The altar boys were leading a procession in which the Archbishop was to follow. Buzz told them after they reached a pretty good height, he would signal them to stoop both the altar boys and the Archbishop, folding their wings in close to their bodies and then attaining their usual speed of 200 mph. When they hit them, incense *thurible,* and processional crucifix went flying, along with *mitre* and a slew of white surplices. "*Mio Dio!*" and "*Ajama!*" were shouted, as the procession stopped, all targeted bent over in pain

Later that day, Buzz made his way into the church as people opened the door to enter it. He hid out in the rafters. When the Archbishop was to consecrate the bread and wine and turn them into the body and blood of Christ, Buzz made his move. He dove down and squirted excrement onto the host and into the chalice.

"Goddamn that bird?" shouted the Archbishop.

There was an audible gasp from the congregation.

"Somebody open the church doors, *poperare!*" he ordered.

They did, and, as Buzz was making his getaway, the Archbishop took off his *mitre* and threw it at him. It missed him by a theoretical mile and landed among the congregation, that big, odd-looking hat covering a small child, pinning her to the pew.

As if it wasn't enough to get a face full of poo on Ash Wednesday, the Archbishop thought. *How will we ever be rid of this bird?*

But, it was only after slipping on his face in excrement going to the rectory in the morning that he decided to take matters into his own hands. He dressed in normal attire and drove out of town so he wouldn't be recognized going into a gun store. He spoke to the owner and decided to spend his congregation's money on an M16, clip and ammo. He had no idea Buzz was in the air watching his every move.

Suspicious, Buzz wondered what he'd want with a gun like that, but decided it was in his best interest to prepare for the worst. So, the next morning, before Rommel woke, he snuck into the German's apartment and stole the shirt of his uniform; it was important that it had all his epauletes on it. Just before sun-up, Buzz was expecting the attack, and it came full force. When the Archbishop saw him cruise by, he pulled out his M16. That's when Buzz flew up with Rommel's shirt and let it go right as the Archbishop started firing. Buzz had been through a gauntlet much worse than this measly priest could produce. When all the smoke cleared, the Archbishop could see that he had put a bunch of 5.56mm sized holes in Rommel's shirt. The Archbishop's eyes stared wide. *What would he do now?* he wondered.

Bazilika Santwarju tal-Madonna ta- Karmnu in Valletta was empty, except for a few elderly ladies with kerchiefs, lighting some candles and on their knees in the pews saying their rosary, their lips moving only. The Basilica of Our Lady of Mount Carmel was where the Archbishop regularly said his Masses. He entered the rectory covertly; afraid he'd be discovered carrying his weapon. He was worried Rommel would come out and see his shirt butchered up so near the church, but he was afraid to pick it up and move it. In the interim, Buzz had taken care of that, placing a bishop's stole, near the shirt he stole, an *omophorion*, to better signal who the shooter was. It worked, too.

After slipping on poo so badly he nearly fell on *his* face, Rommel was furious to find his shirt, and all it stood for, so abused and dishonored

Bang, bang, bang, bang. When Archbishop Conzi opened the rectory door, Rommel rolled out a blistering rant of invective. Conzi hurriedly slammed the door in his face and tried to think of what to do next: gather more of the congregation's money and buy more guns to defend themselves, he decided. He called a special meeting for the men in the parish. Rommel, however had suffered the greatest of all insults. More than a shot-up uniform: a door had been slammed in his face. So, he gathered his men and prepared to go to war against the Catholic Church. Buzz was a happy camper.

Conzi drove the Church men to a gun store. The Mount Carmel Parish men were very uncomfortable at the gun store. They didn't know what they were doing there or what to buy. Archbishop Conzi told them it would be just like shooting play ducks at a carnival stand and placed some high-powered assault rifles in their hands. He bought for them AK-47s, M4s, FN SCARs, M16s, AR-15s, AK-103s, AKMs, IWI Tavors, Koch G36s, AR-18s, *Steyr* AUG, Nr.6 *Galil* and a few like rifles. The gun store owner had to teach them how to load the clips and handle the long guns. They hardly thought these were made for shooting a few duckies at a carnival stand. Later, during a church service, the men were told they may need the rifles to defend themselves and their families against the Germans. This came as a real blow to them. They were speechless and felt like they had been betrayed by their own church. Buzz had gotten into the building by an open door again, chirping and screeching as he jeered at Archbishop Conzi. The Archbishop was made mad by the taunting and opened fire on Buzz, who, again, managed to fly between the bullets. The congregation was stricken with fear. *What kind of a crazed leader do we have?* They wondered what would happen to them next.

Then, it started. "The Luftwaffe and Regia Aeronautica (Italian Air Force) flew a total of 3,000 bombing raids, dropping 6,700 tons of bombs on the Grand Harbor area alone over a period of two years," the radio stated. After a quick breakfast of *balbuljata*, Archbishop Conzi loaded his M16, slipped the clip into the long gun then hurried to his station, again, which was in the "gut" of Malta. No one would think to find him there with the prostitutes, so he remained basically untouched, unless a bomb was dropped there, of course. He'd been lucky so far—his parishioners, not so much. They'd really be upset to hear that since it was his irrational acts that got them into this mess to start with. Buzz was waiting for him today. He knew if he shot up at the falcon, he'd give himself away, so he had to just take Buzz's taunting chirps and screeches and remain quiet, except to give him a finger now and again. He felt like such an ungodly man doing that, but he'd had to do worse since this all started. He actually had to kill a man once, in self-defense, of course. That made it okay to him.

He'd sit there, ignoring Buzz and the artillery fire, day dreaming about the dwarf elephants, dwarf hippos and giant swans that used to be. He wished that he could visit early Neolithic caves like *Ghar Dalam* and see them right then rather than be where he was. He wished there was an easy fix out of this mess. He had to give up saying Mass, of course. Didn't want to give them a target or a time; just needed to lay low and wait it out. His parishioners didn't like it, but he was saving their lives, for Christ's sake. I mean, geez, so ungrateful. About this time Buzz was flying overhead and squirted on his head. That brought him out of his reverie fast. He was so taken aback he jumped up and shot the bird. One lone feather dropped down from above, floating back and forth as it did. Buzz laughed a chirping, screeching laugh. Everything got deathly quiet, then several long guns opened fire in the "gut" of Malta, hitting Conzi right in the leg.

"Ouch! Oh damn, you stupid bird! I'll kill you yet!" He shouted and shook his fist at the sky, then bent over in pain.

Though he was wounded, Conzi shot his M16 in the direction of the German who shot him. Even with his eyes closed he managed to hit him in the heart.

"Okay! I must be living right," he said, "though the pain in my leg hurts so badly it throbs."

At about that time, an Italian plane flew so far down and so close to him that it got stuck in the "gut" of the city. The "gut" had high buildings on either side of a narrow alley. The Italian experienced severe whiplash. It was too funny for Conzi not to laugh, even though he was in pain. When the Italian stuck his head up out of the cockpit, Conzi blew it off.

"That'll teach you." Conzi insisted to preach, even to a headless man.

Hitler didn't spend much time in the theatre with Malta. He was thinking it was taking up more of his time and supplies than it was worth. Buzz had considered the other party in this nightmare, Moose-a-lini, to be a deranged, little-big, misled leader of the Fascist movement He had a hard time being serious about a man with a name like that. As a result, he couldn't be mean to him, He'd cackled just imagining him.

By the time Conzi could seek medical attention, sepsis had settled in. But he had to serve as Archbishop until 1975, so they had to take his leg to save his life. Archbishop Conzi made a hilarious caricature limping around Valletta on his crutches. Buzz almost felt sorry for squirting him when he did. But, "almost" isn't really a feeling.

Buzz was sad that his war with the church had to end with an amputation. He hung around watching Conzi until the cleric was over the phantom leg syndrome. It gave him pleasure knowing he was the source of that ache He learned all about "the" feeling by watching the cleric yearn for his leg. Wishing ConzI still had it, so he could continue to diss him some more, was an itch he couldn't scratch. So, eventually, he had to give it up and go after someone else. He chose Carmelo Borg Pisani, who was a Maltese painter.

Not a cleric, but, oh well, he thought. *Beggars can't be choosers.*

Carmelo Pisani, better known as Borg Pisani, was born into a Maltese Nationalist family in Senglea and became a student at the Italian Umberto Art Lyceum in Valletta in Malta. There he was influenced by Professor Umberto Biscottini and the art camps in Rome. He traveled to Italy to attend the *Accademia di belle arti di Roma* and found other comradery of like ethnic conflicts with his home city-state. Their irredentism was motivated by taking revenge for a previous grievance, such as Italy did with Switzerland and the Austro-Hungarian Empire after 1878, Nazi Germany with Sudetenland in 1938, Somalia's Invasion of Ethiopia in 1977, Argentina's invasion of the Falkland Islands in 1982, attempts to establish a Greater Serbia following the breakup of Yugoslavia in early 1990's, and the Russian annexation of Crimea in 2014. The point is international law is hostile to this type of lawlessness, and Borg Pisani had dug himself in deeper than he should have, especially since that type of lawlessness is a proponent of authoritarian regimes. Irredentism has become a world-wide problem in politics since the mid-twentieth century, causing numerous, unresolved conflicts. It is a significant danger to human security and international order.

"Yes," agreed Buzz, "this is someone I can work with."

Borg Pisani was an impressionist and modern artist. He painted such content as the Madonna, the "glut' of Malta, impressionistic futuristic cities self-portraits, portraits of women seated, and the like. Buzz decided to start with his paintings. That would be the best way to get his goat. Soooo, he decided he'd visit a painting in progress. He flew down to the school and saw that he was creating the Madonna.

That was a reverent painting which would really embarrass him should it be treated irreverently. He flew down low, took careful aim, and squirted the Madonna right in the face. His wet excrement slowly oozed all the way down onto baby Jesus. He flew back, and admired his addition; then, flew up to the rafters and awaited Borg's return. It didn't take long to hear him scream.

"Mio Dio! Cosa hai fatto alla mia arte?!"

Buzz smiled as much as a crooked beak could smile, and then he flapped away to the door waiting for it to be opened.

He next decided it would be rather fun to follow him back to Malta, to see what was so special about Italy besides painting. That's when he realized he wasn't coming home to just see "Mom and Dad." He was coming home to a cave, called *Dingli Cliffs* in *Ras id Dawwara* with a month's worth of rations. As he flew to a ledge to watch what he was up to, he saw him sitting there looking very nervous. Then a monsoonal tide came in and washed all his rations away. He barely got out of there with his life. Soooo, Buzz felt like it would be a real surprise to Borg if Buzz's friends, the dolphins, helped him scrape his rations from the ocean floor and return them to him.

"Mio Dio, da dove vengono questi?"

Borg exclaimed, surprised. *I'll have to thank the dolphins for him,* Buzz thought, and smiled.

This was fun, he thought. *Let's see. What next?* When Buzz heard around town that Borg was a traitor to Malta, and a rising Fascist, he grew sick to his stomach. He needed to do something damaging to him, not help him by saving his rations.

The end result of irredentism is the dissolution of minority rights. Borg Pisani disembarked at the *Dingli Cliffs* in *Ras id-Dawwara* and put his rations there since he knew it from his youth. But, monsoonal tides came up, and had ruined his plans. He had given up his citizenship in Malta, and in May of 1942, volunteered for an espionage mission there. *That's what he was doing in the cave,* thought Buzz, *hiding out from the Maltese police.* So, Buzz alerted authorities that he was back in Malta. He was arrested, tried and sentenced to death by hanging for treason. Buzz kept up with him in the papers. He read that: *The case of Carmelo Borg Pisani periodically returns to the pages of The Times and The Sunday Times as his small cohort of fans try to keep his name burning in the collective memory. This was the case with the article by Laurence Mizzi, which was clear in its intentions and bias. The Borg Pisani case always elicits the same rhetoric. Borg Pisani came back to Malta at the height of the war; intent on collecting information which would have enabled*

Italy to better plan an attack on Malta. Borg was no innocent; he was a Fascist. Mussolini came to power when Borg Pisani was seven, Borg Pisani's only experience of Italy was as a Fascist state, and it was this brand of Italy which he wanted us to come under. Painting him as an innocent (man) is an intentional manipulation of history; he came to take Malta out of British Rule of law and place us under a Fascist country where Jews, Communists and Slovenes were being interned in concentration camps and put to death. Millions of Jews across Europe, as well as homosexuals, Jehovah's Witnesses and many more that had the luxury--they were arbitrarily killed or worked to death by the regimes of Italy and Germany.

Borg Pisani was tried in court by Maltese judges and he was given a sentence established at law; his punishment was not arbitrary, and he would have known the consequences of his actions. And, the clear and unequivocal bias of Borg Pisani's supporters is found in the omission of a very simple detail. Whether in Maltese or in English, I have never come across an author who has ever questioned the fact that he was betrayed by the Italians. *Hmm.* Buzz thought about this. No one knew he was the one who told the authorities. He continued to read.

Thousands of Maltese, my grandparents included, survived those war years *and were proud of their contributions to that victory over fascism.* By constantly banging on about a traitor, we insult their memory and one of the greatest moments in our history. Let Borg Pisani rest in peace with the other Fascists, in the past, never to return.

Buzz put the paper down and wondered how he could have been so duped by this guy. He was really bummed. Now his playtime was really over. No Conzi and no Pisani; the latter had really gotten to him.

The war was supposed to end in a triple bang: shots to the three Allied Nations' leaders' heads: the USSR, Britain and the USA. The plan had been "jump started" by the Soviets to make themselves look good. It was called Operation Long Jump (Unternehmen Weiteptung in German). It was an attempt to assassinate all three of the Allied Leaders, Stalin, Roosevelt and Churchill at a conference in Tehran to be held in October of 1943. It was scrapped by Hitler, who presumably signed off on it to begin with, because he got word the assassins had been found out. It was a theory at best, since no one party would have been together at that place and at that time. It made for a good story telling, though, especially for the USSR, who wrote the book and held the movie rights. Its Code name was Cicero and the German Security Reich supposedly hired the Soviet Skorzeny for their hit man. Yuri Kusnez wrote the book, and Cellia Sandys, Churchill's granddaughter presented the documentary, The Lion and the Bear. Hitler pretty much gave up Malta to Mussolini and focused on the Eastern Europeans. Since it didn't work out that way, the falcons had to work overtime to help end the war. Mussolini and Germany were running out of supplies and fuel there, however.

Buzz's part in the war effort, at this point, started with the ships. He had to have some help creating slippery decks on the Axis ships. His cast brothers did that for him, making a trip to a ship every bowel movement they had. Beyond that, once the boats started firing, Buzz took the brunt of the ducking, zigging and zagging. He was the expert at evading bullets. Buzz also took a great deal of pleasure stooping the crew. At times, when he had to glance off a sailor, he'd take a ride into the depths of the ocean on a friendly dolphin, only to emerge again and soar higher yet for another stoop.

By then, it was time for Buzz to hold another mating-season, cast meeting, to decide how all of this was going to play out. He conferred with Mrs. Peregrine and decided to have a party inside a megalith with German beer to beat them at their own game. So, he ordered several cases of *Rennsteig Boch* to be delivered to *Ghar Dalam*. He had every falcon, both male and female, get slap happy drunk in preparation for the stoop. Some of the falcons swayed out of line a bit on the stoop, but that was to be expected. They righted themselves as the targets neared. They rammed the Germans at a faster 220 mph speed, helmets notwithstanding. The Germans exploded like grenades hit them. Again, he was a happy camper.

Buzz returned to the *Ggantija* Neolithic temples to see what had happened with Mrs. Peregrine and what else she may have in mind.

"Let's just say, I had them both sitting on my arms and wearing hoods," she chuckled.

Buzz chirped and screeched hysterically. "Then what'll you do?" he asked her.

"What I plan to do next is to turn back into a falcon while in their beds. That'll do the trick. Don't you think they'll say eewww then?"

"Oh, I like that," said Buzz. "I like that a lot."

"That should get them to pull out before they are ready to, don't you think? Especially if I let it slip, I've been carrying on with the both of them."

All she heard from Buzz was a bunch of chirping and screeching, accompanied by the bobbing of his whole body.

"You think they'll tell each other what's been going on?" asked Buzz.

"Oh, heavens no. They are much too proud for that. To say they've been hook winked by a woman, much less a bird? I should think not."

"Well, all I can say is you have your claws in their *cajones*. Now all you need to do is finish them off with that pretty hooked beak of yours, my small fragrant flower."

"My plans exactly," she concurred.

When Mrs. Peregrine finally flew home, Mr. Peregrine wanted to know where she had been all that time.

"Oh," she said, "Just making fools of a *fuhrer* and a *comandante.*"

"So, you've been fooling around?"

"Why do you have to make it sound so trashy when all I was doing was getting back at a couple of dict-heads."

"By the way," he said, "you missed mating season."

"Oh darn," she said and flew to her roosting ledge.

Needless to say, the Nazis and Fascists did not win that war. The Allied Forces took out 230 Axis ships in 164 days, the Malti intercepted volumes of German, Enigmatic traffic, and of course, there was "Buzzed flying."

Still, Buzz was very upset with Pisani, He flew back to Ras id Dawwara. Buzz didn't need to be in the Dingli Cliffs caves. He just needed to be at the highest peak of Gozo, facing the west as the sun set. *How can anyone be a traitor to his own country? He knew Malta had been through a lot, but it always came out on top, largely because its people stuck together.* This was new to him. While he was standing there, staring at the beautiful sunset on his beautiful archipelago, he heard a very distinct voice say:

"Here's a sunset for you, kid." As he looked over his shoulder, there in the shadows he saw a falcon with a Borsalino tipped over his eyes.

"Bogie?" he asked.

"Yeh, it's me."

"Well, I'll be," Buzz said elated. "You sure picked a great day to show up. I was beginning to give up on people."

"Oh, don't do that, kid. Never give up on people."

"But this guy was an artist. Okay, yeh, I defiled one of his paintings, but that's no reason to become a traitor. To give up your citizenship and become a Fascist or a Nazi? That's not okay."

"I hear ya, kid. That's not okay."

"So, where ya been, Bogie? Haven't seen ya in a while."

"Been bingeing black and whites," Bogart said.

"That sounds like fun. Not really. What were ya really doing? I was beginning to check the funny papers."

"Ha ha. Been dreaming about Mrs. Peregrine. Had to come and see her," said Bogie, drawing circles in the dirt with a claw.

This was the first time Buzz turned completely around to face Bogie. "Want to see her?"

"I'd love to. But-"

"But what?"

"But what about the 'old man'?"

"Oh, I wouldn't worry about him. She doesn't."

They flew to the mouth of her cave right about dark thirty.

"Wait here," Buzz whispered to Bogie. Mr. Peregrine was already on his roosting ledge fast asleep.

Buzz penguin-walked quietly, trying hard not to let his toe nails scrape on the stone. When he reached Mrs. Peregrine's roosting ledge he leaned over and whispered to her. "I have a surprise for you." She lifted one eye off her sleeping blindfold.

When she saw Buzz, she smiled and lifted the entire blindfold off. He nodded to her to come with him. She followed him to the mouth of their cave. When she saw Bogie, she was so excited she almost couldn't contain herself. He just grinned and they embraced. Buzz waited until their secret meeting was over before he stepped back inside. Bogie crossed beaks with her, and said his usual:

"Here's looking at you, kid," and then he left.

Mrs. Peregrine gave Buzz a hug, thanked him and wished him a good night. It had been that, alright. Bogie coming had, indeed, made it a good night. After all, what could be a better ending than a visit from the Maltese Falcon himself?

Peggy Marceaux

HERE'S TO THE FIN WHALES

Here's to the Fin Whales

HERE'S TO THE FIN WHALES

Joyce woke both nervous and excited, again. Today they would scuttle their fourth *Hvalur* whaling ship in three months. Cold place, but it was the Fin Whales that mattered. She, Mellissa, Isaac and Jeremy hoped everything would run smoothly today. They had been in Iceland now for two weeks getting everything in order. Sinking a ship was no easy matter, but they were staunch activists and weren't easily deterred. She was to meet the men on the wharf near the ship around one this morning.

They hid in the shadows of the wharf lights. "Morning, Jeremy, want some hot coffee? Figured you'd be the first one here," she said in a hushed voice.

"Yeah, thanks. Man, it's cold in this country," he replied, his hands thrust deep in his pockets and his shoulders raised close to him.

She ignored his complaints about the cold. *I mean, they are supposed to bring wetsuits for the swim, so what's the complaint about?* "You've got the tools for the bilge pump and to open the seacocks?" she asked.

"Yeah, I'm just waiting for Isaac so I can give him the wrench for the seacocks. I'm taking care of the bilge pump this time," he said "You and Mellissa gonna bring the sloop in closer? That's cold water to swim in, even with wet suits on," and he shivered.

She turned around, perused the darkness while taking a sip of her coffee. *Looks like a little storm's brewing out there.* She was pretty fed up with Jeremy's ambivalence; then she turned back to him, needing him. "Sure, we know the drill. We can't get much closer, Jeremy, or they'll be on to us. Just try not to worry so much," she worked to assure him. "Now listen, I know I've told you and Isaac this before, but it is very important we get everyone; we can't let a boat go overboard to harpoon a whale. Not even one"

"Yes, we understand, Joyce. Can't let a harpoon get away. We got that."

When Isaac arrived, dressed as a deck hand to Jeremy's seaman, Jeremy handed him the wrench for the seacocks, and then they turned to go.

Joyce stopped them. "Isaac, I see you brought your flash light. How 'bout you, Jeremy? You're not going to have these wharf lights down there like you do out here."

"Gosh, guess I'm a mess today. I forgot it."

"Here, take mine," and she handed Jeremy her flash light. "Don't forget to leave them the National Resources Defense Council's --**our** calling card," she smiled, and handed them a copy of *Moby Dick*. "Leave it in the wheel house, under a chart. That way it'll buy us enough time to get the job done."

"Oh, yeah, forgot to ask for it," stated Isaac. When they turned to leave, she told them "Good luck."

They both made their way up the ship's ramp and onboard. Isaac sneaked over to the wheel house to leave the book then, together, they slipped down into the hull and out of sight. When the ship pulled up anchor and untied at the dock, all seemed to go as planned--no one got found out, and no one found *Moby Dick* ahead of time, or they would have known something was amiss. The ship hit heavy squalls and deep water fast. The little schooner watching them was trying to survive the squalls itself, losing a little time because of them.

Jeremy and Isaac had long since found their sea-legs, otherwise, this would be a nauseous ride. The squalls were unrelenting for the first half hour. Finally, when things settled down a bit, before long, they heard, *"Hvah jo, erfitt ao hafna!"* They knew enough about Icelandic by now to know that they said "Whale ho, hard to port side," which meant they needed the man in charge of the rudder to turn it hard to the port or left side, because the whale was on the starboard or right side. They had quickly ditched their clothes for their wet suits when they felt they wouldn't be discovered, and now it was time for the real work. Jeremy jammed the bilge pump up so it couldn't be used, and Isaac opened all the seacocks. Water flooded into the hull more than a gallon a seacock a second. Isaac and Jeremy went topside and got lost in the general melee of men gathering the harpoons and loading them with grenades to explode the in the bellies of the whales on the starboard side, of the ship. They made their way to the port side and slipped into the icy water. The schooner sat farther away than Jeremy wanted it to be; he had no choice but to swim to it.

Before the whalers could get their smaller boats to chase the whale and get a harpoon shot off, they realized they were sinking. Someone ran down to the hull and came up calling for help. By now, the open seacocks had done their job, and the whalers knew they'd been scuttled. They couldn't budge the bilge pump so there was no way they could pump out the water. Suddenly the helmsman thought of that *Moby Dick* novel under the chart. He remembered another ship master telling him about the NRDC leaving it as a "calling card" for another scuttled ship.

"Fjandinn!" (Damn!) he exclaimed, and got on the horn: *"mai, mai, mai"* (mayday, mayday, mayday), he called.

Meanwhile, the Americans reached the schooner—Isaac first. Jeremy was noticeably blue when the women and Isaac pulled him up the ladder. He sat there and shivered so badly his teeth chattered. Even when they gave him hot coffee, he was having trouble not spilling it. When they looked out at the whaling ship they could see it going down. The whalers had all put their lifeboats on the water and were climbing in, waiting for rescue.

"Job completed successfully," said Joyce; she and Melissa high fived and turned the schooner around, headed to their safe inlet on the far side of the dock. While sailing into their harbor, Joyce remembered the last time it wasn't completed successfully. It was three years ago to the day when she, Melissa, her husband, Zach, and their friend,

Jeff, had been commissioned by the NRDC to scuttle a Japanese whaler in the Sea of Japan. She couldn't think of the Japanese in any other way now but inhumane, despite what they do to the Fin Whales. Once Zach and Jeff had jammed the bilge pump and opened the seacocks so that water would flood into the hull, they were caught. The sea captain had ordered his men to batten down the hatches so Zach and Jeff couldn't get out; they drowned as a result. Joyce had to do some real soul searching after that to decide whether this vocation were really worth it. All it took, though, was looking at yet another Fin Whale and its calf being hauled up by Japanese tackle near a sign on the stern of their whaler that read it was being done all "in name of science." Zach's drowning had crushed her. She became visibly ill and stayed that way for days, lost to the world and living only in her own thoughts. She eventually gave all his clothes away, yet she couldn't part with his favorite jacket. She wore it almost every day for the northern scuttles. She saved her crying for nighttime while alone in bed. She just couldn't believe the Japanese had done that to him, although they knew that was always a risk, and they seemed eager to take it on "for the Fin Whales." If she ever had the chance to, she knew she would pay them back somehow.

The next day she received their next NRDC commission, this one for Norway.

"Another cold country," said Jeremy.

Joyce turned to him. "Are you sure you volunteered for these scuttles?" Joyce asked him. "Most all of them are in cold countries?"

Jeremy hung his head. "Yes, I did. I just didn't think about that part of it. I'm not sorry I did, though. I like what we're 'doing. My body doesn't, but my mind truly believes in it."

"Well, Oslo, Norway's Norwegian's Sea is next. You may want to do a little homework on it before we go, but we'll be scuttling the. Kato early in the morning of the 7th; it'll be hunting blue whales," Joyce informed him; If you want to trade the bilge pump for seacocks, now's the time to tell Isaac."

"No, I'm okay with my job," he remarked. "Where'd you get that jacket? Seems warm."

"It is," answered Joyce, "and my husband's cologne permeates it."

"Oh--I didn't realize. I apologize."

"No apologies necessary. You'd just have to skin me alive to get it off me," she answered with a smile.

As she made her way back up to her hotel room, she ran into Melissa coming down the elevator going to breakfast.

"You've already had breakfast?" she asked.

"Not really hungry." Joyce answered

"Aw, c'mon now, Joyce, you have to eat something. You can't just let old memories stop you in your tracks." Melissa challenged her.

Joyce turned to her. "I hardly call what happened to Zach an 'old' memory."

"Okay, I apologize for that, but you can't let what happened *then* keep you from eating *now*," Melissa clarified.

"I eat when I'm hungry."

"Okay. Have it your way. But I'm going to sit down to some eggs and bacon," Melissa tempted her.

"You do that," deflected Joyce. "I'll be in my room," and she headed for the elevator.

That night she took out all of the items in the drawer she brought of Zach's: a silver money clip with a couple of twenty-dollar bills, a picture of her, a picture of their three-year-old-daughter they lost, a name badge from the NRDC and a picture of his brother with Down's Syndrome. He never took them with him on a job for just the reason that happened to him. She prized those possessions, especially the picture of Emily. Emily had been only two-years-old when she developed Glioblastoma. Only two years old, with a brain tumor, plus a cancerous one at that; how can parents deal with such a thing? It was the worst year of their lives. *Don't know what Zach and I would have done had we not had one another for comfort,* she thought. That last year of Emily's life had been heart breaking for both Joyce and Zach. After losing Emily, losing Zack tore her heart out. She wanted the chance to scuttle another Japanese ship. But she was patient; for now, it would be the Kato. The blue whale was a cousin to the Fin Whale – a hybrid cousin. Both endangered, it made her sick they were hunting them.

She shied away from company that night, and walked over by the quay. It was breezy, most of the ships were in and tightly secured to the bitts. She walked to see if she could find the Kato, just to see if it would put in in the same place each night. This information would be important to them the morning they planned to enter the ship. She found it; it was almost at the end of the quay. She searched for it the next night and found it in its same spot. She would check each night for a week, just to be sure

The next morning, Joyce awoke fresh, though, heavily laden with memory. She dreamed last night of Zach and Emily. She didn't want to get out of bed for fear of losing them again, but she had an eight o'clock appointment with the crew downstairs at the café, so she knew she had to get up. She donned Zach's jacket, as a finishing touch, along with her pair of fur-lined boots, and started down the elevator. They were all waiting for her in the café.

"Morning, guys," she greeted them.

"Morning," they mumbled, or said, each with his or her own lack of enthusiasm. Jeremy had not been looking forward to another freezing swim, but what was the matter with Isaac and Melissa?

"Oh, oh, I detect a problem." Joyce responded.

"The schooner has a sail that has torn away from the bottom of the mast. It'll take them another week to repair it," Melissa said with her head down.

"Besides putting us off schedule, that's not so big a problem," Joyce replied. They all looked up, surprised, but relieved. That wasn't at all like Joyce. Normally; she would have been very upset.

After breakfast, Joyce followed Melissa down to their wharf to see exactly what the problem was with the sail. She saw the tear for herself, and agreed that the schooner was not able to sail. While down there, she walked around to the main quay, which was quite a distance in a big circle, and checked out the spot for the Kato; she found it empty, but that wasn't unusual for the time of day. They would have put out much earlier than 9:30. The point was the spot was empty, waiting for her return, which was good.

She walked back up to her hotel and took the elevator back to her room. She picked up *Moby Dick* and continued to read it for the fourth time in her life. Each time, she found some reason to pull for the white, Sperm Whale that Ahab, the captain of the Pequod, hated. She had left off on page, 290, where it speaks of carving up the smaller whales like the Right Whales. The Sperm Whales, the author, Melville, compares to Leviathans:

When severed, the head is dropped astern and then held there by a cable until the body is stripped. That done, if it belongs to a small whale it is hauled on deck to be deliberately disposed of, but, with a full-grown leviathan, this is impossible; for the sperm whale's head embraces one third of his entire bulk and completely to suspend such a bulk as that, even by the immense tackles of a whaler, this were as vain a thing as to weighing a Dutch barn in jeweler's scales.

The Pequod's whale being decapitated and the body stripped, the head was hoisted against the ships side—about half way out of the sea, so that it may yet in part be buoyed by its native element. And there with the straining craft steeply leaning to it, by reason of the enormous downward drag from the lower mast-head, and every yardage on the side projecting on that side like a crane over the waves; there that blood-dripping head hung to the Pequod's waist....

When the last task was completed, it was noon, and the men went below to their dinner. Silence reigned over the tumultuous but now deserted deck. An intense copious (abundant) calm... more and more was unfolding its noiseless measureless calm upon the sea.

A short space elapsed, and into this noiselessness came Ahab alone from his cabin. Taking a few turns on the quarter-deck, he paused to gaze over the side, then slowly getting into the main-chains he took Stubb's long spade—still remaining there after the whale's decapitation—and striking it into the lower part of the half-suspended mass, placing its other end, crunch-wise under one arm, and so leaning over with eyes attentively fixed on this head.

This passage was one of Joyce's favorites, for it depicted the depravity of the whaling industry as a whole, no matter what the century, and Ahab's mad-man's vengeance for his lost leg specifically; however her very favorite passage was yet to come: Moby Dick meeting that vengeance head on, which, of course, one must read for oneself. Remembering how it ended lulled Joyce to sleep with a smile, still wearing Zach's jacket and cradling Emily's picture. One week passed pretty quickly with her reading most of the time, and she was fairly sure Jeremy was getting acclimated. The morning she was supposed to meet the men came; she remembered it felt like she had only past by the bed the night before rather than sleeping. She didn't even need to set an alarm for 1:00. When she went down to the quay, Isaac was the only one waiting for her.

Herman Melville, Moby Dick (New York: Bantam, 1981) 290.

"What's up, Isaac? Where's Jeremy?"

"He skipped town," Isaac answered.

"You're kidding me?" She was furious. "He could have told me that for at least a week."

"I know," he said. "I had nothing to do with it. I tried to talk him out of it."

"Oh, I believe you," she said. Metaphorical smoke was coming out of her ears, she was so hot!

"Look, I don't want to postpone this again. Let me get a wet suit, tell Melissa what's going on, and then I'll join you back down here," she told him.

"Oh, Joyce, I don't know if it's such—"

"No. Don't try and stop me, Isaac. I can hold my own with the best of you."

He turned and looked off, then, turned back again. "Okay," he reluctantly stated.

"I've got the bilge pump," she said.

"That's good, because I think the seacocks would kick your butt."

"As well, I don't mind cold water, and I have a wonderful breast stroke," she said smiling. "Also, I have the copy of *Moby Dick* to leave in their wheelhouse," she told him.

"Well, I've got the bilge pump tool," he said.

"Okay; I'll hurry."

Melissa was horrified that Joyce was even thinking of doing something like this. Yes, she knew she had been a swimmer in college and had done pretty well for herself. But here, in the subzero waters of Norway? Melissa became angrier and angrier at Jeremy for not giving them time to search for someone else. She hoped he had a conscience, and that the guilt ate him alive.

"Yes, Joyce. I can operate the schooner without you just this this once. The waters are smooth, and it's forecast to stay that way through tomorrow." Melissa assured her.

"Then let's get going before it's too late," Joyce urged her.

Joyce had donned some workman's clothes and tied her hair up when she got her wet suit and met

Isaac at the wharf to the get the bilge tool. "It's a go," she said," and they hurried up the ramp. Joyce quickly stopped by the wheel house to place *Moby Dick* under a chart, then, they entered the hatch toward the hull, turned on their flash lights and made their way down to the very belly of the ship. They changed into their wet suits and waited patiently to feel the whaler go out to sea and hear the whalers holler that they'd spotted a whale. They didn't have to wait long, maybe thirty minutes, before the excitement started:

"Hval ho, vanskelig a styrbord!" A seaman shouted.

"The whales on the starboard side," she told Isaac.

"Yeah, the chaos will be there. Let's slip off the port," he stated in a hushed tone.

"There's the bilge pump" Isaac pointed and whispered, then made his way to the seacocks. Joyce watched him place the wrench on one and paid attention to the way he had to strain to open it. He didn't strain at all. She needed to remember how to put the wrench on it so she wouldn't have to strain either. Then, she pulled up the bilge handle and rigged it so it couldn't be pulled up, or pushed down; it was jammed in place. In the meantime, Isaac had all the seacocks open, and water was beginning to pour in by the gallons.

"Let's get outta here," Joyce told him.

They slipped over the fore-to-the-port side of the ship while all the seamen were on the other side rigging the harpoons. Within seconds, Joyce and Isaac were out of sight. The water was, indeed, icy, and though their extremities were numb, they managed to swim toward Melissa and the schooner. Isaac, however, suddenly, developed a cramp in his leg, so Joyce had to cross-chest carry him in. It was a harrowing experience, but it gave Joyce the confidence she'd need for scuttling the Japanese whaler in the future. As they climbed, or were pulled aboard, the schooner, they watched the seacocks do their job, and the whaler go down before they could kill another whale. The Norwegians were all climbing in their lifeboats as the schooner turned and sailed away.

Another success, she thought and smiled while she shivered. *Bye, bye Kato,* she thought. Hot coffee in a thermos wasn't enough. She needed a hot bath, Zach's warm jacket, and plenty of hot chocolate.

Joyce and Melissa went to eat out to celebrate their success at a well-known restaurant in Norway. Isaac had to beg off because he wasn't feeling well. He had a headache and symptoms of the flu. The girls sure hoped it wasn't COVID. The flu would be bad enough because they couldn't wear masks to swim. They kept him in mind and hoped for the best, telling him they would check on him later in the evening. Joyce ordered a bottle of Stag's Leap Artemis, a wonderful cabernet that Zach had loved. They each ordered *escargot* for an appetizer and a leafy green salad with the house dressing, which came with sourdough bread. Melissa ordered lobster to Joyce's mix of clams and crab meat. Melissa was excited to see Joyce eat. She felt the tide had finally turned for her.

They truly expected to be stationed in Norway for a while, but the NRDC said the Kato whalers had spotted the schooner at sea when they were climbing into their lifeboats. The company wanted to pull them out of there as soon as possible. So, that very night, they were packing their bags. All but, Isaac, that is. He was too ill to be moved just now. Melissa, Joyce and the schooner were placed in the Sea of Japan. Melissa was worried Joyce would be upset about where they had been sent, but she seemed, not only resigned, but grateful to be there. Melissa didn't understand it, but she was glad this didn't throw her back into bad memories again. Not only did it not throw her back into her bad memories, but she was more than happy to see that the first whaler they had to sink was the Nisshin Maru, the same whaler in which her husband had drowned. Melissa was thrown by Joyce's behavior. She didn't understand it.at all

Three days later, Melissa and Joyce were walking along the harbor, looking for some kind of inlet or cove deep enough for the schooner to hide. They found one.

"But, Joyce, I'm worried about you having to swim all this way," Melissa told Joyce.

"Oh, this isn't far at all. I have a nice, easy breaststroke that I can use to swim all day long if I want. It's not a problem. And, the waters here aren't nearly as cold as they are in those northern countries," Joyce replied

"Well, I suppose you know what you are doing," Melissa said.

In three more days, Joyce had herself all ready to go. She had convinced Melissa she didn't need Isaac to help her out, since she had watched him open the seacocks, and it hadn't been difficult at all. She was dressed as a seaman and had her hair put up under a cap in a bun. She had taken Zach's and Emily's pictures, Zach's jacket with Moby Dick in one the pocket and the flash light in the other, the bilge pump jammer and the seacocks wrench. She also had a small Greenwork's drill that was both battery-operated and silent she had bought at Home Depot. She told Melissa she'd meet her at the schooner at their usual time.

She made her way up the ramp to the Nisshin Maru at one in the morning. They only had twelve men working this ship, so she didn't have many lifeboats, but with the drill, she scuttled them all, making inconspicuous holes throughout the soles (the bottom boards). Then she hid in the hull; Joyce didn't bring a wet suit, because she had no reason to change into one. She waited and continued to read Moby Dick by flash light.

The four whales slain that evening had died wide apart; one far to the windward (facing the wind); one, less distant, to leeward (in the calm); one ahead; one astern (to the back). These last three were brought alongside ere nightfall; but the windward one could not be reached till morning; and the boat that had killed it lay by its side all night; and that boat was Ahab's.

The waif-pole (a pole that marks a dead whale in the sea as belonging to some someone) was thrust upright into the dead whale's spout hole; and the lantern hanging down its top, cast a troubled, flickering glare upon the black, glossy back and far out upon the midnight waves, which gently chafed the wale's broad flank, like soft surf upon a beach.

Ahab and all his boat's crew seemed asleep but the Parsee (Persian astrologist) who crouching in the bow, sat watching the sharks that spectrally played round the whale and tapped the light cedar planks with their tails....

Started from his slumbers, Ahab, face to face, saw the Parsee; and hooped round by the gloom of the night they seemed the last men in a flooded world. "I have dreamed of it again," said (Ahab) he.

"Of the hearses? Have I not said, old man, that neither hearse nor coffin can be thine?"

"And who are hearsed that die on the sea?"

"But I said, old man, that ere (before) thou couldst die on this voyage, two hearses must verity (truly) be seen by thee on the sea; the first not made by mortal hands; and the visible wood to the last one must be grown in America."

"Aye, aye! a strange sight that, Parsee;--a hearse and its plumes floating over the ocean with the waves for the pallbearers. Ha! Such a sight we shall not soon see."

"Believe it or not, thou can't not die till it be seen, old man?..."

"I have two pledges here that say I shall yet slay Moby Dick and survive it."

Now in that Japanese sea...the warmest climes but nurse the cruelest fangs...tornadoes (that have) never swept northern isles. So, too, it is, that in these resplendent Japanese seas the mariner encounters the direst of all storms....

"Why sing ye not out for him, if ye see him? When after the lapse of some minutes since the first cry, no more had been heard." Sway me up, men; ye have been deceived; not Moby Dick casts one odd jet that away, and then disappears.— "

The triumphant halloo of thirty buckskin lungs was heard as much nearer the ship as the imaginary jet, less than a mile ahead—Moby Dick bodily burst into view! For not by any calm, and indolent spoutings; but by the peaceable gush of the mystic fountain in his head, did the White Whale now reveal his vicinity; but by the far more wondrous phenomenon of breaching --in an act of defiance.

"Aye, breach your last, to the sun, Moby Dick!" cried Ahab. "Thy hour and thy harpoon are at hand."

It was at this point that Joyce heard the mariners board the Nisshin Mura "Aye, your hour and you harpoon are at hand, Nisshin Mura. I've waited three long heart-breaking years for this." Joyce mumbled to herself.

Herman Melville, Moby Dick (New York; Bantam, 1981) 450-4, 461, 505.

None of the men sounded alarmed, so they must not have noticed the scuttled life boats. That's good, she thought. Someone opened the hatch to the hull and looked down. He even came down and looked around. Joyce hid in the shadows. She had forgotten to take her novel with her, but reached for it quickly; he saw her, but she hit him hard over the head with the bilge tool. He looked like he was really bothered by having been given this job, but she quickly dispensed of him. She was a bit unnerved that he had discovered her, but she smiled at her response.

Finally, she guessed the men had unmoored the ship because it was moving slightly. Then. it started moving at a pretty good clip. When she next looked at her watch, she realized they were already forty-five minutes into their hunt when she finally heard the cry: "Kujira senbi de kara!"

She knew *kara* meant stern. She kept watch on the Japanese whaler in the hold with her. The first thing she did was close and lock the hatch from the inside. Then she jammed the bilge pump so they couldn't pump any water out; she went to the seacocks to see how difficult they were to open. You had to struggle a bit more here than Isaac had, but they weren't as bad as the plumbing under her sink. So, she opened all of them and let the sea water pour in by the gallons. She could hear some men calling out by now, so she knew some of them had discovered the scuttled lifeboats.

There was a lot of commotion going on up there, even some banging on the hatches. Finally, she heard the captain's call for help:

"*Mede mede mede.*" The Japanese sailor revived in all the water coming in. He tried to fight his way to the hatches and open them. Joyce hit him on the head again to put him out of her misery. *He needed to drown like she and Zach,* she had decided. The captain sounded his mayday over and over again. *I don't think all of his men could be saved,* she thought. As the water started to engulf her, strangely, she was surprised her body struggled to live when her mind was so set on dying. She was also surprised that her last thoughts weren't of Zach or Emily. They were of Melissa waiting for her in the sloop.

About the Author
Peggy Marceaux

Peggy Marceaux is a retired English teacher who lives in Canyon Lake, Texas. She earned her Bachelor's Degree from Lamar University and her Masters of Arts from the University of Houston, where she specialized in British Literature.

Ms. Marceaux taught for 32 years; 11 in the Alvin Independent School District and 15 in the Comal Independent School District in TX, Chairing the High School English Departments in both.

Having raised chickens for twenty years, she loved the diversity among the breeds. This inspired "BeakSpeak", a story designed to help young people accept their differences and build confidence, through speech validation. Ever the English teacher, Ms. Marceaux believes the earlier you teach children language precision, the better it will help them succeed in their future relationships and careers.

Along with BeakSpeak, Ms. Marceaux is also involved with CLAW the Canyon Lake Area Writers at the Tye Preston Memorial Library in Canyon Lake, Texas where they meet for two hours the first and third Tuesday of each month. They enjoy letting their creative juices flow with writing prompts, have visiting speakers import helpful knowledge, and submit their 5,000-to-8,000-word short stories to Raconteur in the hopes of gaining publicity.

Short Story Collections:

About BeakSpeak – the Characters

The BeakSpeak characters are inspired from Peggy's own chickens! Some 30+ years ago Peggy began raising chickens on her farm and discovered that chickens have personalities. Along with their very personable characteristics they must learn quickly that there is a pecking order. Like human society, some chickens behave aggressively, others passively, and weak birds cannot survive a bully without a human intervening.

Her chicken coop, then became the English classroom, where Ms. Marceaux taught language skills for 32 years in high school. "My greatest reward was watching my students grow to respect one another, find their confidence, learn how to rationally think about the world around them, and then shape their views to fit in that world. I was able to help them do all this by teaching them that, when you think, speak and write precisely and concisely, using the clearest and most effective words, with the most energetic verbs to defend your views, the better you communicate your meaning."

The first BeakSpeak book is a colorful rendition of a classroom of chickens who are learning about thinking and language skills. Add to those techniques, Marceaux stimulates thought with her exploratory questions, and suggested answers. BeakSpeak, A Fable and Language Workbook is a perfect companion piece with this book as everyone can benefit from learning how to better communicate with others!

These books are available anywhere books are sold online. Learn more on **www.PeggyMarceaux.com**

Erin Go Bragh Publishing publishes various genres of books for numerous authors. Their portfolio consists of a 1200-page Vietnamese to English Dictionary, Historical fiction, an award-winning children's educational series, and an array of fun children's picture books, multiple adult novels and memoires, tween adventure stories, as well as Christian Fiction. Their objective is to promote literacy and education through reading and writing.

www.ErinGoBraghPublishing.com
Canyon Lake, Texas